THIS WALKER BOOK

BELONGS TO:

. . . .

. . . .

To Katie

First published 2003 by Walker Books Ltd
87 Vauxhall Walk, London SE11 5HJ

This edition published 2008

2 4 6 8 10 9 7 5 3 1

© 2003, 2008 Charlotte Voake

The right of Charlotte Voake to be identified
as author/illustrator of this work has been asserted by her in
accordance with the Copyright, Designs and Patents Act 1988

This book has been typeset in Calligraphic.

Printed in China

British Library Cataloguing in Publication Data: a catalogue
record for this book is available from the British Library

ISBN 978-1-4063-1270-6

www.walkerbooks.co.uk

GINGER
finds a home

Charlotte Voake

WALKER BOOKS
AND SUBSIDIARIES

LONDON · BOSTON · SYDNEY · AUCKLAND

Once there was
a little ginger cat
who lived in
a patch of weeds
at the bottom
of a garden.

His ears were black
with dirt. He was very thin.
His fur stuck out.

His tail was like
a piece of
STRING!

He drank water
out of puddles.
He looked in dustbins
for things to eat.

Every day he searched
for food,
and every night,
he went back
to his patch of weeds
to sleep.

Then one day,
everything
changed.

The little cat had found
nothing to eat except
a bit of bread,
and he was cold
and hungry as he
came back to bed.

He stopped.
There on the
ground was ...

a delicious
plate of
cat food!

He couldn't believe his eyes!

He gobbled it up
and went to sleep.
He had never
slept so well!

The next night,
he found another
plate of food
waiting
for him ...

and SOMETHING
ELSE.

A little
girl!

"Hello,"
she said.

She tried to stroke his fur,
but he was
frightened,
and ran
to hide
in the
weeds.

"See you tomorrow,"
said the little girl.

She came to visit
him every day.
She brought him
lovely things
to eat.

She
called him
Ginger.

Soon Ginger looked
forward to seeing
the little girl.
He came when
she called, and when
she stroked him,
he purred.

The little girl loved Ginger.

"Ginger," she said.
"You can't stay here.
Why don't you
come home
with me?"

So Ginger followed
the little girl
home.

He had never
been in a house before.

He looked
in all the
corners and
under all
the furniture.
But poor
Ginger
was
so nervous ...

that when the little girl
tried to shut
the door,

he ran out into
the garden as fast as he could.

The little girl
looked outside.
She couldn't
see him
anywhere.
"Ginger!"
she called.

But Ginger didn't come.

"I've frightened
him away,"
she said.
"He doesn't
want to
live with
me."

The little girl
was very sad.
She was so upset,
she didn't notice ...

when Ginger came
creeping back in.

"Miaow!"

said Ginger.

"GINGER!"

said the little girl.

Now Ginger
lives with
the little
girl in her
house.

He is a very
happy cat.

And the only time
    he ever goes back
    to the patch of weeds
        at the bottom
            of the garden ...

is to
sunbathe!

Charlotte Voake

The work of Charlotte Voake is renowned throughout the world for its gentle wit, quiet observation, airy exuberance, and charm. Winner of the **Smarties Book Prize** for *Ginger*, Charlotte says of her work, *"I just draw with ink, over and over again – until I think, 'Aha, that's how it should be!'"*

ISBN 978-1-4063-1269-0

ISBN 978-1-4063-1270-6

ISBN 978-1-4063-1271-3

ISBN 978-1-4063-1272-0

ISBN 978-1-4063-0714-6

ISBN 978-1-4063-0523-4

ISBN 978-0-7445-8958-0

ISBN 978-1-4063-1405-2

Available from all good bookstores